INTERIORS

First published 1987 by GMP Publishers Ltd,
    PO Box 247, London N15 6RW
This collection copyright © GMP Publishers 1987
Text copyright © Emmanuel Cooper 1987
Pictures copyright © Cornelius McCarthy 1987
French translation by Elizabeth Ganne
German translation by Christiane Bergob

British Library Cataloguing in Publication Data

McCarthy, Cornelius
    Interiors: paintings.
    1. McCarthy, Cornelius
    I. Title
    759.2   ND497.M2/

    ISBN 0-85449-037-X
    ISBN 0-85449-015-9 Pbk

Photoset by MC Typeset Ltd, Chatham, Kent, England
Photography by Harold Rose
Colour origination, printing and binding by
    South Sea International Press Ltd, Hongkong

INTERIORS

PAINTINGS BY

CORNELIUS McCARTHY

INTRODUCED BY
EMMANUEL COOPER

Introduction

Cornelius McCarthy is very much an artist of our time. His work is figurative and his subject matter, more often than not, is the nude and semi-nude male, often centred on the complexities and dilemmas of modern urban life. The ambiguities and contradictions with which the artist deals are reflected in the title of the collection 'Interiors'. This refers not only to the fact that much, though not all, of his work is set inside buildings, but more importantly to the 'interiors' his paintings invite us to explore. The close and personal relationships suggested in the paintings have a psychological interior in which the investigation of inner thoughts and feelings goes beyond external appearance.

Since he first started painting some 30 years ago, Cornelius McCarthy's style has developed slowly but consistently. His painting has continued to reflect a sensitive awareness of the

Introduction

Cornelius McCarthy est un artiste bien de notre époque. Son oeuvre est figurative et ses sujets sont le plus souvent des nus masculins – et à demi vêtus – souvent au centre des difficultés et des embarras de la vie citadine moderne. Les ambiguïtés et les contradictions dont traite l'artiste sont reflétées par le titre de la collection: "Interiors". Ceci se réfère non seulement au fait qu'une bonne part de son oeuvre – sinon toute – se situe à l'intérieur d'habitations, mais encore et surtout aux "intérieurs" que ses tableaux nous invitent à explorer. Les rapports intimes et privés suggérés dans ces tableaux ont un intérieur psychologique dans lequel l'étude des pensées et des sentiments intimes va au-delà des apparences.

Depuis qu'il s'est mis à peindre il y a une trentaine d'années, le style de Cornelius McCarthy s'est formé lentement mais dans la continuité. Sa façon de peindre n'a cessé de refléter

Einführung

Cornelius McCarthy ist in vieler Hinsicht ein zeitgemäßer Künstler. Sein Werk ist figuratif und seine Thematik dreht sich hauptsächlich um Akt oder Halbakt, wobei diesen Arbeiten häufig die Verflechtungen und Schwierigkeiten des modernen Stadtlebens zugrunde liegen. Die Widersprüche und Vieldeutigkeiten, mit denen sich der Künstler beschäftigt, werden in dem Titel der Serie 'Interiors' angedeutet. Das geht nicht nur aus der Tatsache hervor, daß sich die meisten seiner Darstellungen im Innern von Gebäuden abspielen, sondern auch ganz besonders aus den Interieurs, die zu Entdeckungen einladen. Die engen, persönlichen Beziehungen, die in den Bildern angedeutet sind, haben ein psychologisches Innenleben, das von Auseinandersetzungen mit tiefen Gedanken und Gefühlen zeugt, die über die Äußerlichkeiten hinausgehen.

Da Cornelius McCarthy vor circa dreizig Jahren damit

long traditions of the western figurative humanist tradition, particularly that which developed in Renaissance Italy some 500 years ago. He has also been aware of other contemporary artists whose concerns seem to be close to his own, particularly at a time when abstract rather than figurative art was in favour.

As a young student at Goldsmiths' College, London (when he was only 15) Cornelius McCarthy came under the formative influence of Sam Rabin, a painter and sculptor who taught him life drawing. Rabin was greatly respected by many of his students, and a measure of his importance to Cornelius McCarthy is suggested by the fact that the young student carefully preserved the teacher's instructive demonstration drawings carried out on the edges of his own work. A small recently acquired painting ('*The Young Prospect*' p. 6) by

Sam Rabin –
The Young Prospect

une perception aigüe des vieilles racines de la tradition figurative de l'humanisme occidental, surtout celles qui doivent leurs origines à l'Italie de la Renaissance il y a près de 500 ans. Il est également conscient des autres artistes contemporains dont les préoccupations semblent proches des siennes, en particulier à une époque où l'art abstrait, plutôt que l'art figuratif, jouissait de la préférence.

Jeune étudiant au Goldsmiths' College de Londres (il n'avait que 15 ans), Cornelius McCarthy subit l'influence formatrice de Sam Rabin, peintre et sculpteur qui lui enseigna à peindre d'après nature. Rabin était très admiré de ses élèves, et on peut juger de l'impact qu'il eut sur Cornelius McCarthy quand on sait que le jeune étudiant a conservé soigneusement les croquis explicatifs dessinés par le maître dans le marges de ses propres dessins. "*The Young Prospect*" (p. 6), un petit

tableau de Rabin que Cornelius McCarthy a récemment acquis, est accroché chez lui. L'accord intense mais tendre entre les deux personnages est rendu avec sensibilité, mais il est facile de se rendre compte que la force de cette oeuvre, quoique très différente dans ses intentions, se rapproche des thèmes propres à Cornelius McCarthy.

De Rabin, Cornelius McCarthy a appris la discipline d'observer et de rechercher la ligne correcte pour l'équilibre et les volumes. De telles préoccupations sont plus celles d'un sculpteur que d'un peintre, et pourtant Cornelius McCarthy est toujours conscient des formes du personnage. La couleur, pour aussi vitale qu'elle soit à sa peinture, leur cède le pas. De l'enseignement classique de Rabin, auquel se sont ajoutés des encouragements judicieux, Cornelius McCarthy a tiré les moyens d'exprimer ses propres aspirations.

begann zu malen, hat sich sein Stil langsam aber gezielt entwickelt. Seine Malerei zeugt durchgehend von einem sensitiven Bewußtsein, daß die lange Geschichte der westlichen, figurativen, humanistischen Tradition – insbesondere die der italienischen Renaissance vor rund 500 Jahren – widerspiegelt. McCarthy war sich aber auch anderer zeitgenössischer Künstler bewußt, dessen Anliegen seinem eigenen nahe schienen und das zu einer Zeit, in der die abstrakte Kunst der figurativen allgemein vorgezogen wurde.

Als junger Student am Goldsmiths' College, London (er war erst 15), wurde Cornelius McCarthy formal von Sam Rabin beeinflußt, einem Maler und Bildhauer, der ihn im Aktzeichnen unterrichtete. Rabin fand große Anerkennung unter seinen Studenten, wie wichtig er für Cornelius McCarthy war, zeigt sich darin, daß der junge Student die

skizzierten Anleitungen seines Lehrers auf den Rändern seiner eigenen Arbeiten verwahrte. Ein kleines, kürzlich erstandenes Gemälde von Rabin ('*The Young Prospect*' s. 6), hängt in McCarthys Haus. Das Bild vermittelt die starke aber sensibile Beziehung der beiden dargestellten Figuren sehr einfühlend, aber es ist offensichtlich, daß auf ganz die Stärke seiner Arbeit, wenn auch auf ganz anderer Ebene, eine thematische Ähnlichkeit mit Cornelius McCarthys eigenen Arbeiten aufweist.

Cornelius McCarthy lernte von Rabin die Fähigkeit, auf die korrekte Linienführung sowohl als auf Ausgewogenheit und Schwerpunkt zu achten. Solche Belange sind eigentlich mehr Sache des Bildhauers als des Malers, aber dennoch bleibt sich Cornelius McCarthy stets der Form des Dargestellten bewußt, und obwohl Farbe eine wichtige Rolle in seinen

Rabin hangs on the wall of Cornelius McCarthy's house. The powerful but tender relationship of the two figures in the painting is sensitively expressed, but it is not difficult to see how the strengths of this work, though very different in intention, come close to Cornelius McCarthy's own themes.

From Rabin, Cornelius McCarthy learnt the discipline of looking and searching for the correct line, for balance and weight. Such concerns are more those of the sculptor rather than the painter, and still Cornelius McCarthy is ever conscious of the form of the figure. Colour, however much a vital part of his painting, is subservient to it. In Rabin's classically based teaching Cornelius McCarthy found a means of expressing his own ideas, encouraged by sensible advice.

In one of Cornelius McCarthy's early paintings 'Ray as a Saint in a Landscape' (p.15) completed when he was 20, there are all the beginnings of his 'style'. The scale is small, the medium gouache (one he uses very often) lends itself particularly well to this size: it does not present the physical handling difficulties of oil paint, and is particularly convenient when studio space is restricted. Stylistically the figure blends into the background, colour and tonal values suggest integration of subject and context. There is little attempt to create the illusion of perspective or depth. Cornelius McCarthy's use of colour is to flatten rather than extend the picture, to intensify the richness of the image rather in the way of religious icons, and to make us aware of the artifice of the artist. The subtle use of decorative patterns to break up the background both blends and binds the figures. Similar devices are used to good effect in 'Mick with Man in Leather' 1982 (p. 28) and 'David, Henry and Hoddle' 1984 (p. 45).

Dans l'un de se premiers tableaux, "Ray as a Saint in a Landscape" (p. 15), qu'il acheva quand il avait 20 ans, on retrouve toutes les ébauches de son "style". Les dimensions sont modestes et la gouache – qu'il utilise très souvent – s'y prête particulièrement bien: elle ne présente pas les difficultés de manipulation de la peinture à l'huile et convient en studio quand l'espace est restreint. Le personnage se fond styliquement dans le décor; des valeurs de couleurs et de nuances suggèrent l'intégration du sujet et du contexte. Il a peu cherché à créer l'illusion de la perspective ou la profondeur. Cornelius McCarthy utilise la couleur pour aplanir plutôt que pour prolonger l'image, pour intensifier la richesse de l'image à la façon des icônes et pour nous rendre conscients de l'habileté de l'artiste. L'usage subtil de motifs décoratifs pour briser le décor de fond mélange et lie les personnages en même temps. La même technique a été employée avec succès dans "Mick with Man in Leather", 1982 (p. 28), et "David, Henry and Hoddle", 1984 (p. 45). On y remarque aussi un intérêt pour la religion et la beauté du modèle masculin. Ray, malgré son halo, n'est pas un saint: son esprit est fermement ancré en ce bas monde plutôt que dans l'autre.

Le début des années 60 marqua un tournant significatif dans la peinture de Cornelius McCarthy: ce fut quand il alla voir une grande rétrospective de Keith Vaughan à la Whitechapel Gallery de Londres et en fut profondément impressionné. Bien qu'il connaisse déjà l'oeuvre de Vaughan, l'occasion de voir ses tableaux en masse et de suivre le cours de sa pensée eut une importante influence sur lui. Pour la première fois, il se rendait compte du fait qu'il n'y avait pas besoin de justifier le choix du nu masculin comme sujet.

Bildern spielt, ist sie dieser Tatsache unterworfen. Durch Rabins klassische Art des Unterrichts fand Cornelius McCarthy, unterstützt von hilfreichem Rat, einen Weg seine eigenen Ideen zu verwirklichen.

In einem frühen Bild McCarthys, daß er mit 20 machte, nämlich 'Ray as a Saint in a Landscape', (s. 15), finden sich alle seine 'Stile'. Die Skala ist eher klein und die Mittel der Gouachemalerei, (die er sehr oft benutzt), eignen sich besonders gut für diese Größe: sie haben nicht die physischen Schwierigkeiten in der Handhabung von Ölfarbe und sind besonders praktisch bei limitiertem Platz im Studio. Stilistisch gesehen verschmeltzen die Figuren mit dem Hintergrund, und Farbe und Tonwerte suggerieren die Integration von Subjekt und Kontext. Es wird nicht versucht eine Illusion von Perspektive und Tiefe zu schaffen.

Cornelius McCarthy benutzt Farbe eher zum verflachen als zur Erweiterung des Bildes, er benutzt Farbe, um damit die Fülle des Dargestellten wie bei einer religiösen Ikone zu intensivieren und um den Betrachter auf die Künstlichkeit des Künstlers aufmerksam zu machen. Der subtile Gebrauch dekorativer Muster um den Hintergrund aufzubrechen, verbindet und verschmelzt die Figuren zur gleichen Zeit. In 'Mick with Man in Leather' (s. 28) und 'David, Henry and Hoddle' 1984 (s. 45) sind ähnliche Muster mit gutem Effekt benutzt worden. In McCarthys Bildern gibt es neben einem religiöses Anliegen auch das der Schönheit des männlichen Körpers. Ray ist trotz seines Heiligenscheins kein Heiliger, seine Aufmerksamkeit gilt ja vielmehr dieser Welt als der nächsten.

Ein Haupteinfluß auf Cornelius McCarthys Arbeiten übte in

There is also a concern with religion and the beauty of the male figure. Ray, despite the halo, is no saint; his mind is firmly directed towards this world rather than the next.

A major influence in Cornelius McCarthy's painting came in the early '60s when he saw and was deeply impressed by the large retrospective exhibition of Keith Vaughan at the Whitechapel Gallery, London. Though aware of Vaughan's work, the chance to see his painting in quantity, and to follow the development of ideas, had a profound effect. For the first time Cornelius McCarthy became aware of the fact that it was not necessary to justify taking the male nude as a subject.

For a period Cornelius McCarthy's work ran close to that of Vaughan's; subjects were similar and figures were broken into abstract squares and oblongs, often painted with a broader, more physical awareness of the pigment. It is useful to compare the strange group of men in 'Harlequins – The Meeting' 1963 (p. 16) and 'Three Nudes' (p. 18) – a much less emotive title – painted shortly afterwards. One, posed in an eerie half-light, depicts figures involved in some unstated though clearly significant event; there is a narrative involvement. In the other, the group has no recognisable activity, it becomes an event much more of the artist's making: the figures though in close physical proximity seem psychologically apart; the painting too is broader with the flattened, square-edged brush marks making full use of the thick qualities of the oil pigment. The artist is now in charge of the subject, there is a new confidence, a bolder assurance.

With the series of portraits painted a few years later, Cornelius McCarthy had successfully absorbed the ideas of Vaughan. These portraits are 'real' people, some such as 'The

---

Pendant un temps, la peinture de Cornelius McCarthy suivit de près celle de Vaughan; les sujets étaient similaires et les personnages brisés en formes abstraites carrées et oblongues étaient souvent peints avec une conscience plus large et plus physique de la matière colorante. Il est utile de comparer l'étrange groupe d'hommes dans "Harlequins – The Meeting", 1963 (p. 16) et "Three Nudes" (p. 18) – au titre moins accrocheur – peint peu de temps après. L'un, baigné d'une étrange pénombre, dépeint des personnages engagés dans une activité indéterminée quoique manifestement significative: il y a un engagement narratif. Dans l'autre, le groupe n'exerce pas d'activité reconnaissable, et l'action vient davantage de la main de l'artiste: bien que très proches physiquement, les personnages semblent séparés psychologiquement. La peinture est plus appuyée avec des coups de brosse à plat et carrés, utilisant à fond la densité de la peinture à l'huile. L'artiste maîtrise désormais son sujet et montre une confiance réelle et une assurance plus hardie.

Avec la série de portraits peints quelques années plus tard, Cornelius McCarthy a assimilé avec succès les principes de Vaughan. Ces portraits sont des gens "vrais"; certains, comme dans "The Paisley Shirt", 1971 (p. 21) par exemple, évoquent classe sociale et personnalité. Le titre distrait presque du sujet principal du tableau: ce Mod avec sa coiffure à la mode et la cravate nouée négligemment. Nous sommes très conscients de l'attrait physique du personnage, une qualité qui est rendue de la même façon – sinon encore plus fortement – dans "Young Harry Boy", 1979 (p. 29). La pose est provocante et le blouson de cuir, le jeans et les bottes évoquent une forte présence sexuelle.

---

den frühen 60er Jahren die große Retrospektive von Keith Vaughan in der Whitechapel Gallery, London, aus. Denn obwohl ihm Vaughans Werk bekannt war, machte erst die Gesamtheit der gezeigten Arbeiten und die Möglichkeit, dem Gedankenaufbau des Künstlers zu folgen, einen tiefen Eindruck auf ihn. Zum ersten Mal erkannte Cornelius McCarthy die Tatsache, daß es nicht unbedingt nötig ist, den männlichen Akt zum Thema zu nehmen.

Eine Zeit lang ähnelten Cornelius McCarthys Arbeiten denen von Vaughan; die Themen waren ähnlich und die Figuren waren in abstrakte Quadrate und Rechtecke aufgebrochen, oft waren auch die Arbeiten derber in der Ausführung und ziegten ein größeres körperliches Bewußtsein für Pigmente. Es ist interessant die seltsame Männergruppe in 'Harlequins – The Meeting' 1963 (s. 16) und 'Three Nudes' (s. 18) – ein Bild das kurz darauf entstanden ist und einen viel emotionsloseren Titel hat, zu vergleichen. Das eine ist in einem etwas unheimlichen Halblicht gehalten aus dem sich Figuren, die in irgendein, wenn auch unklares Geschehen verwickelt sind, hervorheben – es hat einen erzählerischen Inhalt. In dem anderen zeigt die Gruppe keine erkennbare Aktivität, sondern wird vielmehr zu einer, vom Künstler gestellten Begebenheit: Die Figuren scheinen – obwohl körperlich nah – geistig fern voneinander; das Bild ist auch breiter und macht sich mit abgeflachten, kantigen Pinselstrichen die dickliche Konsistenz der Ölfarbe zu nutzen. Der Künstler beherrscht jetzt sein Thema, seine Arbeitsweise zeugt von mehr Vertrauen, von einer stärkeren Selbstsicherheit.

Ein paar Jahre später machte Cornelius McCarthy dann

Paisley Shirt' 1971 (p. 21) for instance, evoke social class and character. The title almost deflects from the major subject of the painting, that of the Mod with his fashionable hairstyle and casually knotted necktie. We are very aware of the physical attractions of the figure, a quality which is equally if not more strongly expressed in 'Young Harry Boy' 1979 (p. 29). The pose is provocative, the black leather jacket, jeans and boots evocative of a powerful sexual presence.

Within the last 10 years two major themes have arisen in Cornelius McCarthy's painting, though often there is a rich cross-over. One is with figures, either naked or clothed, either in pairs or in groups, often set in a domestic interior and locked in some deep and mysterious involvement. The other is the religious paintings in which the figures not only portray events and emotions, but comment very directly on the times in which we live.

One of the artists Cornelius McCarthy most admires is Picasso – not I would hazard a guess for the spirited eclecticism of this great artist but rather his ability to express a particular sort of freedom. This draws on the traditions of art, and on subject matter in such a way as to give the artist complete control whilst still acknowledging a historical and cultural debt. There is something of this freedom in Cornelius McCarthy's own approach. 'Mandy and Bill with Floral Curtain' 1979 (p. 26) contrasts the naked and the clothed figure: the integration of pattern and surface through careful choice of colour is a sensual setting for the ambiguous relationship. Is his look questioning or desiring? Is her averted gaze playful or rejecting?

In 'Mick with Man in Leather' 1982 (p. 28), both male figures

---

Au cours des dix dernières années, deux grands thèmes se dégagent de la peinture de Cornelius McCarthy même si souvent, ils se recoupent avec opulence. Le premier, ce sont des personnages nus ou vêtus, par paires ou en groupes, souvent représentés dans un intérieur domestique et engagés dans quelque action mystérieuse et absorbante. L'autre, ce sont des tableaux religieux dans lesquels les personnages non seulement indiquent des actions et des sentiments, mais témoignent aussi d'une manière très directe sur l'époque dans laquelle nous vivons.

L'un des artistes que Cornelius McCarthy admire le plus est Picasso mais pas, à mon avis, pour l'éclectisme vigoureux du grand peintre, plutôt pour son génie à exprimer une qualité particulière de liberté. Elle s'appuie sur les traditions artistiques et sur le sujet, de façon à donner à l'artiste le contrôle total tout en rendant hommage au passé historique et culturel. On retrouve quelque chose de cette liberté dans l'approche de Cornelius McCarthy. "Mandy and Bill with Floral Curtain", 1979, oppose le personnage nu et vêtu: l'intégration du motif et de la surface grâce au choix méticuleux des coloris constitue une mise en scène sensuelle pour ces rapports ambigus. Son regard à lui est-il inquisiteur ou amoureux? Elle, les yeux baissés, se fait-elle désirer ou le rejette-t-elle?

Dans "Mick with Man in Leather", 1982 (p. 28), les deux personnages masculins s'étreignent plus intimement, plus étroitement, avec peu de distance entre eux, physique ou spirituelle. Leurs rapports sont sexuels, intimes et tendres, avec un élément de taquinerie, de jeu. La pose de Mick, à demi couché, à demi vautré, soumis, détendu, invite l'ardeur et l'admiration, et peut-être aussi le désir. La manifestation

---

eine Serie von Porträts, in denen er Vaughans Ideen erfolgreich absorbierte. Diese Porträts zeigen 'echte' Menschen, einige davon, wie zum Beispiel 'The Paisley Shirt' 1971 (s. 21), behandeln Gesellschaftsschichten und deren Verhalten. Der Titel lenkt in gewisser Weise von dem Hauptthema des Bildes ab, nämlich dem des 'Mod' mit seinem modischen Haarstil und der lässig gebundenen Krawatte. Man ist sich der körperlichen Reize der Figur bewußt, eine Fähigkeit McCarthys, die schon in 'Young Harry Boy' 1979 (s. 29), stark zum Ausdruck kommt. Die Pose ist provokativ; schwarze Lederjacke, Jeans und Stiefel kreieren ein starkes sexuelles Moment.

Innerhalb der letzten zehn Jahre haben sich zwei Hauptthemen in Cornelius McCarthys Arbeiten herauskristallisiert, obwohl es häufig kreativ Überlagerungen gibt. Das eine Thema behandelt Personen: entweder nackt oder bekleidet, manchmal in Paaren, manchmal in Gruppen; oft in häuslicher Umgebung und versunken in irgendwelche dunklen und mysteriösen Geschehen. Das andere Thema dreht sich um religiöse Bilder, in denen die dargestellten Personen nicht nur Ereignisse und Gefühle porträtieren, sondern auch direkten Bezug zu der Zeit in der wir leben nehmen.

Einer der Künstler, die Cornelius McCarthy am meisten bewundert, ist Picasso. Aber man könnte annehmen, daß es ihm dabei eher um die Fähigkeit dieses großen Künstlers geht, eine bestimmte Art von Freiheit auszudrücken, als um dessen geistigen Eklektizismus. Das bezieht sich also auf die Thematik, insofern es dem Künstler völlige Kontrolle gibt und dabei dennoch geschichtliche und kulturelle Bezüge berücksichtigt. Cornelius McCarthy hat etwas von dieser Freiheit in seiner Arbeitsweise. 'Mandy and Bill with Floral Curtain' 1979 (s. 26),

are more closely, more intimately locked together with little distance, either physically or emotionally between them. Their relationship is sexual, close and tender yet with an element of teasing, of playfulness. Mick's pose, half lying, half lolling, subservient, relaxed, is one which invites warmth and admiration as well as, perhaps, lust. The physical display is also an emotional vulnerability. The pose, which echoes the figure of Christ in Michelangelo's Pieta (St Peter's, Rome) occurs again in other paintings, most notably in 'Boy and Nude with Head Thrown Back' 1985 (p. 47), 'Harry in Socks with Nude' (p. 10) and 'XIII Belfast Station of the Cross – Pieta with Banner' 1982 (p. 10). The prone naked figure is particularly striking in contrast to the clothed, and therefore, much more concealed figures. In all the paintings the emotional charge is high, the relationships complex, hinting at sexual intimacy, emotional

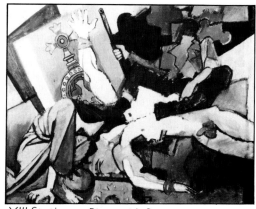

Harry in Socks with Nude

physique traduit aussi la vulnérabilité des sentiments. Cette pose, qui rappelle celle du Christ dans la Pietà de Michel-Ange à Sainte-Pierre de Rome, se retrouve dans d'autres tableaux, en particulier dans "Boy and Nude with Head Thrown Back", 1985 (p. 47), "Harry in Socks with Nude" (p. 10), et "XIII Belfast Station – Pieta with Banner", 1982 (p. 10). Le nu allongé sur le ventre est particulièrement frappant face aux personnages vêtus et donc beaucoup plus dissimulés. Dans tous les tableaux, le climat émotif est intense, les rapports complexes, suggérant l'intimité sexuelle, la dépendance sentimentale et la force qui peut s'en dégager.

Mais il n'est pas de lecture simple de l'oeuvre de Cornelius McCarthy: ce qui à première vue paraît clair s'avère à l'étude beaucoup plus complexe. Que penser par exemple de "Tottenham Interior", 1982 (p. 38), ou de "Spent Star –

XIII Station – Pieta with Banner

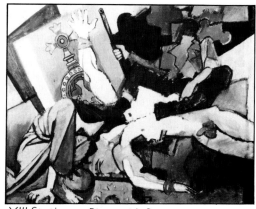

kontrastiert den nackten und den bekleideten Körper: die Integration von Muster und Oberfläche durch bedachte Farbsetzung, schafft eine sinnliche Komposition dieser ambivalenten Beziehung. Ist sein Blick fragend oder begehrend? Ist ihr avertierter flüchtiger Blick spielerisch oder ablehnend?

In 'Mick with Man in Leather' 1982 (s. 28), sind die beiden männlichen Personen näher und intimer zusammengebracht – mit wenig physischer oder emotionaler Distanz zwischen ihnen. Ihre Beziehung ist sexueller Natur, nah und zärtlich aber doch mit einem scherzenden, spielerischen Element. Micks Haltung, halb liegend, halb rekelnd, unterwürfig und entspannt, vermittelt Wärme und Bewunderung aber vielleicht auch Lust. Die körperliche Zurschaustellung hat auch etwas von einer emotionellen Verletzbarkeit. Die Pose, die die Darstellung von Christus in Michelangelos Pieta (St. Peters,

Rom) wiederholt, taucht auch in anderen Bildern auf, ganz besonders in 'Boy and Nude with Head Thrown Back' 1985 (s. 47), in 'Socks with Nude' (s. 10) und in 'XIII Belfast Station – Pieta with Banner' 1982 (S. 10). Die vornüber geneigt, nackte Figur bildet einen sehr starken Kontrast zu den bekleideten und deshalb viel versteckteren Figuren. Der emotionale Moment ist in allen Bildern sehr stark, die Beziehungen scheinen verwickelt, deuten auf sexuelle Intimität und emotionale Abhängigkeit und dadurch auf die Stärke, die daraus erwachsen kann.

Aber Cornelius McCarthys Werk ist nicht so eindeutig: was auf den ersten Blick offensichtlich erscheint, kann sich beim näheren Hinsehen als sehr viel verstrickter erweisen. Wie soll man zum Beispiel 'Tottenham Interior' 1982 (s. 38), oder 'Spent Star – Koblenz' 1985 (s. 58), interpretieren? Beide sind

10

dependence and the strength this can give.

But there are no single readings of Cornelius McCarthy's work: what at first seems clear proves much more complex on investigation. What for instance do we make of 'Tottenham Interior' 1982 (p. 38), or 'Spent Star – Koblenz' 1985 (p. 58)? Both are small in scale, with richly detailed painting, and both have the intensity in treatment and in subject matter of a Russian icon. None of the figures direct their look at each other; there is a post- rather than a pre-coital mood, an air of uncertainty pervades – we are seeing a past as well as a future. In these and other recent paintings one of the major concerns is the enigmatic relationships between men.

Some of these ambiguities occur in the series of religious paintings 'The Belfast Stations of the Cross' (p.31–34).The subject is one which artists have painted for hundreds of years, and all have brought their own feelings. The relationship between the sacred and the secular, a topic which was hotly debated by the neo-Platonists in Italy, is one of the underlying concerns of Cornelius McCarthy's painting.

Of his religious paintings 'Belfast Pieta with St. Therese' 1983 (p. 35) stands out, not only for its complex composition, its carefully orchestrated emotional impact, but above all for its lament on the horrors of war and violence in our own time. The figure of Christ who we identify with the besieged city dominates the scene; he lies diagonally, his head tenderly supported by his mother. By his hand there is a spilt chalice; behind there are the rich designs of an altar cloth; a chorus of women gaze at the dead Christ with deep-felt sorrow. In the background thick plumes of smoke indicate the carnage of war. The mood is one of compassion and reflection, though

Koblenz", 1985 (p. 58)? Les deux tableaux sont petits, avec une palette très richement détaillée et tous deux ont subi l'intensité de traitement et de sujet d'une icône. Aucun des personnages ne regarde l'autre; on sent un climat d'après l'amour plutôt qu'y préludant, il règne un air d'incertitude – nous contemplons un passé aussi bien qu'un avenir. Dans ces tableaux et d'autres plus récents, l'une de ses grandes obsessions concerne les énigmatiques rapports entre hommes.

Certaines de ces ambiguïtés se retrouvent dans la série de tableaux religieux intitulée "The Belfast Stations of the Cross" (p. 31). Le sujet a été peint par des artistes depuis des siècles et tous y ont apporté leur propre part d'émotion. Les rapports entre le sacré et le séculaire, objet de chaudes discussions par les Néo-platoniciens en Italie, sont l'une des préoccupations sous-jacentes dans les tableaux de Cornelius McCarthy.

Parmi ses tableaux religieux, "Belfast Pieta with St. Therese", 1983 (p.35), se détache des autres, non seulement en raison de sa composition compliqué et de son impact émotif soigneusement orchestré, mais par dessus tout pour ses lamentations sur les horreurs de la guerre et la violence de notre époque. Le personnage du Christ que nous identifions avec la ville assiégée domine la scène; il est étendu de travers, la tête tendrement soutenu par sa mère, un calice renversé à côté de la main. Derrière, on voit les riches motifs d'une nappe d'autel; le choeur des femmes contemple le Christ mort avec une profonde tristesse. En arrière-plan, d'épais nuages de fumée indiquent le carnage de la guerre. Le climat tend à la compassion et à la réflexion, mais pas au désespoir – à travers la mort, nous trouverons la vie et la paix succède à la

kleinformatig und weisen reich detaillierte Malerei auf, beide haben in der Behandlung die Intensität einer russischen Ikone – das trifft auch auf die Thematik zu. Keine der dargestellten Personen sehen sich an; es hat eher etwas von einer nach- als vorkoitalen Stimmung, es liegt eine Unsicherheit in der Luft – man sieht eine Vergangenheit sowohl als eine Zunkunft. In diesen anderen kürzlich entstandenen Bildern ist eines der Hauptanliegen die enigmatische Beziehung zwischen Männern.

Diese Ambivalenz taucht teilweise auch in den Serien religiöser Bilder auf 'The Belfast Stations of the Cross (s. 31). Das Thema wurde schon seit Hunderten von Jahren von Künstlern aufgegriffen und alle haben ihre eigenen Gefühle eingebracht. Die Beziehung zwischen Sakralem und Säkularem – einem Thema, das schon von den Neo-Platonisten in Italien heiß diskutiert wurde – ist eine der unterschwelligen Problematiken mit denen sich Cornelius McCarthys Bilder beschäftigen.

'Belfast Pieta with St. Therese' 1983 (s. 35) hebt sich unter seinen religiösen Bildern nicht nur ob seiner komplexen Komposition und seiner bedacht orchestrierten emotionellen Eingabe, ab, sondern vor allen Dingen durch seine Anklage der Schrecken durch Krieg und Gewalt in unserer Zeit. Die Christusfigur, die man mit der belagerten Stadt erkennen kann, dominiert die Szene; er liegt diagonal, sein Kopf wird zärtlich von seiner Mutter gestützt. Neben seinen Händen ist ein umgestoßener Kelch, dahinter die reichverzierten Tücher eines Altars; ein Frauenchor wirft einen mit tiefer Trauer erfüllten Blick auf den toten Christus. Im Hintergrund deuten dichte Rauchschwaden das Blutbad des Krieges an. Die

not despair – through death we may find life, after violence peace. Disturbing elements within the painting reflect those of war itself; the appalling destruction, the seemingly mindless killing, the suggestion of salvation through pain and even death, and the contradictions with religious belief. The Belfast Pieta is far from being a conventional religious painting yet its meditative theme and moving compassion make it suitable for any church.

Paintings in 'The Belfast Stations of the Cross' are set against a war background. In 'XI Station – The Victim is Nailed' 1982 (p. 32) the naked, vulnerable and broken figure of Christ is contrasted by the sheer brutality of the soldier. Interestingly, despite the dominating position of the soldier and his dark anonymous presence, it is a white, muscular but prone Christ figure who seems to be winning the battle. In other religious paintings there is a mixing together of emotional and physical passion, of the sacred and the profane, of love and lust. There are suggestions that there are choices to be made, decisions to be taken; the implication is that just as the artist takes control of the painting, so we can take some control of our lives.

Emmanuel Cooper

violence. Des éléments troublants dans le tableau reflètent ceux-là mêmes de la guerre; l'effroyable destruction, la tuerie apparemment insensée, la suggestion du salut par la douleur et même par la mort, et les contradictions dans les croyances religieuses. La "Belfast Pieta" est bien loin d'être un tableau religieux classique et pourtant, son sujet recueilli et sa compassion touchante le rendent digne de figurer dans une église.

Les tableaux de la série "The Belfast Stations of the Cross" sont peints sur fond de guerre. Dans "XI Station – The Victim is Nailed", 1982 (p. 32), le corps nu, vulnérable et brisé du Christ contraste avec la brutalité absolue du soldat. Il est intéressant de noter qu'en dépit de la position dominante du soldat et de sa sombre présence anonyme, c'est le corps du Christ, pâle, musclé mais allongé, qui semble remporter la victoire. Dans d'autres tableaux religieux, il y a un mélange de passion physique et spirituelle, de sacré et de profane, de charité et de désir. Il y a la suggestion que des choix sont à faire, qu'il faut prendre des décisions; l'idée est que, tout comme l'artiste s'octroie le contrôle de sa peinture, nous devons nous octroyer le contrôle de nos existences.

Emmanuel Cooper

12

Stimmung ist voller Mitleid und Reflektion, aber ohne Verzweiflung – durch Tod mögen wir vielleicht Leben finden, nach Gewalt vielleicht Frieden. Beunruhigende Elemente innerhalb des Bildes spiegeln sich im Krieg selbst; die verheerende Zerstörung, das scheinbar sinnlose Töten, die Suggestion von Heil durch Schmerz und sogar Tod und die Widersprüche im religiösen Glauben. Die Belfast Pieta hat wenig mit einem herkömmlichen religiösen Bild zu tun, doch könnte es ob seines meditativen Themas und ob des ergreifenden Mitleids in jede Kirche passen.

In den Bildern 'The Belfast Stations of the Cross' stellen die Hintergründe Krieg dar. In 'XI Station – The Victim is Nailed' 1982 (s. 32), bildet die nackte, ausgelieferte und gebrochene Figur Christi den Gegensatz zu der schieren Brutalität der Soldaten. Interessanterweise ist es die weiße, muskuläre, aber vornüber gebeugte Figur Christi, die trotz der dominierenden Position des Soldaten und dessen dunkler anonymer Präsenz, den Kampf zu gewinnen scheint. In anderen religiösen Bildern gibt es eine Mischung von emotioneller und physischer Leidenschaft: ob sakral und profan oder ob von Liebe und Lust. Hier wird angedeutet, daß es zu wählen gilt – daß Entscheidungen getroffen werden müssen; mit anderen Worten: so wie der Künstler sein Bild unter Kontrolle nimmt, so können wir unser Leben kontrollieren.

Emmanuel Cooper

PAINTINGS BY

CORNELIUS McCARTHY

Ray as a Saint in a Landscape   1955

13 × 15 cm

gouache

16

Harlequins – The Meeting   1963

24.5 × 32 cm

gouache

Three Nude Bathers   1963

25 × 30 cm

oil on panel

Three Nudes 1963

35 × 30 cm   oil on panel

Four Nudes   1963

35 × 23 cm   gouache

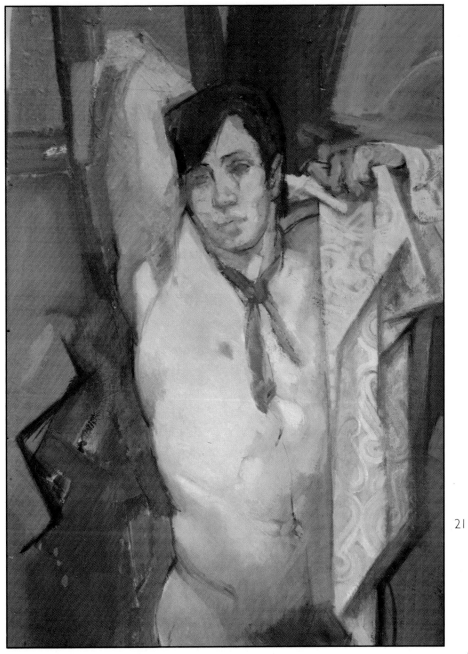

The Paisley Shirt   1965

92 × 63.5 cm   oil on panel

Colin With William Against a Window   1969

39.5 × 30 cm   oil on canvas

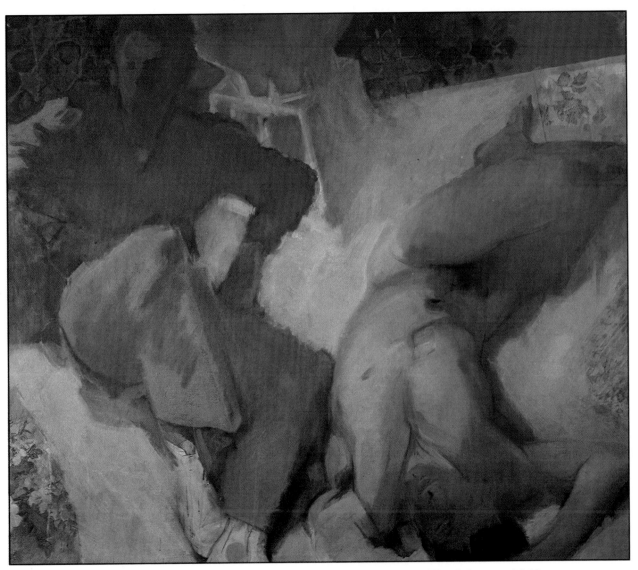

Two Figures – Tunisia   1969

109 × 124.5 cm

oil on canvas

Group of Grey Figures   1964

24.5 × 33 cm

gouache

Mandy and Bill Against a Floral Curtain   1979

34.5 × 34.5 cm   oil on canvas

Kazak – Shore Leave   1982

63 × 50 cm   oil on canvas

Mick With Man in Leather   1982

151 × 181 cm

oil on canvas

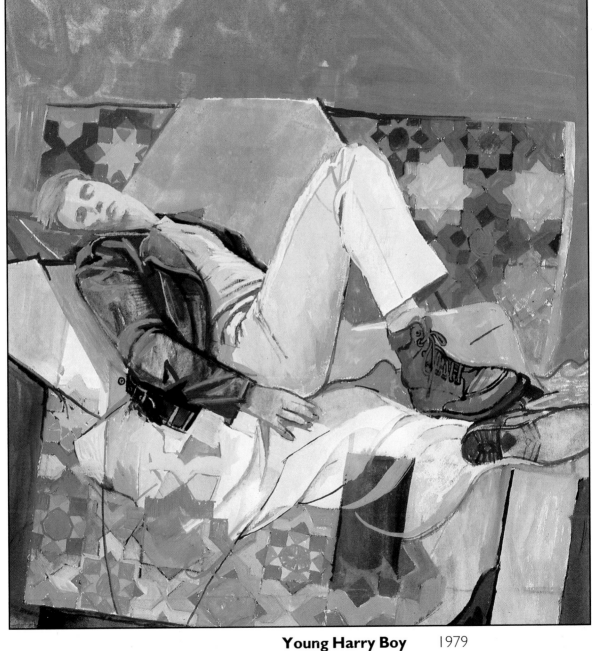

Young Harry Boy   1979

25 × 23 cm   gouache

XIII Pieta with Gunman   1982

12.5 × 12 cm   gouache

32

XI The Victim is Nailed   1982

27 × 23 cm   gouache

IX The Third Fall   1982

27 × 22.5 cm   gouache

33

34

VIII The Women   1982

29.5 × 23 cm   gouache

Belfast Pieta With St. Therese 1983

70 × 90 cm

oil on canvas

David and Clive   1984

45 × 45 cm   oil on canvas

Tottenham Interior I   1982

21 × 23 cm

gouache

Young Harry Boy With Naked Friend   1979

14 × 14 cm   gouache

Red-Head With Nude   1983

24 × 24.5 cm   gouache

Mick Tied by E.P.   1984

39 × 29 cm   gouache

David With Reclining Nude   1984

28 × 36.5 cm

gouache

David With Standing Nude   1984

36.5 × 26 cm   gouache

44

Two Against a Pink Pattern 1979

19.5 × 17 cm gouache

David, Henry and Hoddle   1984

27 × 29 cm

gouache

46

E.P. With Nude   1983

30 × 27 cm   gouache

Boy and Nude With Head Thrown Back   1985

30 × 23 cm   watercolour

Bathers in a Wood   1982

26 × 31 cm

gouache

50

The Park – Black Bathers   1985

75 × 75 cm   oil on canvas

Johnny's Friends   1985

24 × 26 cm   gouache

53

Limehouse Dawn   1985

126 × 100.5 cm   oil on canvas

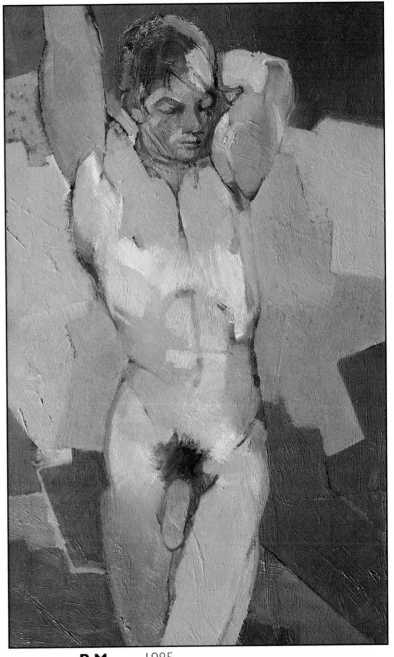

P.M. 1985

52 × 30 cm   oil on canvas

Clive With Man Who Looks Like Paul   1985

31 × 23 cm   watercolour

Two Figures With Cubist Still Life   1985

23 × 22 cm   gouache

Spent Star – Koblenz   1985

45 × 39 cm   gouache

Nude and Man With a Rope   1985

48 × 38 cm   gouache

Nudes With Neo-Classical Cloth   1985

33 × 34.5 cm

gouache

Johnny With White Boy   1985

12.5 × 12.5 cm   gouache

Index

Fine Art Books from GMP

Philip Core
PAINTINGS: 1975–1985
Introduced by George Melly
40 colour plates

Mario Dubsky
TOM PILGRIM'S PROGRESS AMONG THE CONSEQUENCES OF CHRISTIANITY
Introduced by Edward Lucie-Smith
64 b/w plates

Juan Davila
HYSTERICAL TEARS
Edited by Paul Taylor
35 colour plates

David Hutter
NUDES AND FLOWERS
Introduced by Edward Lucie-Smith
40 colour plates

Michael Leonard
PAINTINGS
Foreword by Lincoln Kirstein
The artist in conversation with Edward Lucie-Smith
40 colour plates

Michael Leonard
CHANGING
Introduced by Edward Lucie-Smith
50 b/w plates

Douglas Simonson
HAWAII
40 colour plates

Nick Stanley
OUT IN ART
Featuring work by gay artists
Christopher Brown   Chris Corr   Norman Richard Boyle   Graham Ward
37 colour plates

Art Photography

George Dureau
NEW ORLEANS
Introduced by Edward Lucie-Smith
50 duotone plates

Wilhelm von Gloeden
TAORMINA
Introduced by Emmanuel Cooper
20 b/w plates

Full catalogue available on request from
GMP Publishers Ltd, PO Box 247, London N15 6RW